"THE HIDDEN GEM OF FOREST"

YASIR MUHAMMED S

This book is dedicated to all those who face adversity with unwavering determination, who turn challenges into stepping stones toward a brighter future. It is dedicated to the dreamers who refuse to be defined by their circumstances, the resilient souls who find strength in the face of adversity, and the compassionate hearts that give back to the world.

To the Alexys of our world, whose stories inspire us to chase our dreams relentlessly and to make a positive impact on the lives of others. This book is for you, and it is a testament to the extraordinary potential that resides within each of us, waiting to be discovered and shared with the world.

May the pages within serve as a source of inspiration, encouragement, and hope, reminding us all that no matter where we come from or what challenges we may face, our capacity for resilience and the pursuit of our dreams knows no bounds

Contents

Foreword

In the following pages, you will embark on a remarkable journey—an odyssey of determination, dreams, and the enduring strength of the human spirit. The story of Alexy, a young boy from a remote village near the forest, is a testament to the boundless potential that resides within us all.

This book invites you to witness Alexy's life unfold, from his modest beginnings in a close-knit family to the challenging days in a technical school, and from the depths of his emotional struggles to the pinnacle of his achievements as a multi-billionaire entrepreneur. It is a story that takes you on a rollercoaster ride of emotions and experiences, a journey that resonates with the universal themes of hope, resilience, and the pursuit of dreams.

As you turn the pages, you will come to know Alexy not only as a character but as an embodiment of the human capacity to overcome adversity. His path is marked by hardships, moments of self-doubt, and the pain of loss, but it is also illuminated by the unwavering support of family and friends, the power of mentorship, and the transformative force of love.

In the end, this book is a celebration of resilience—the strength to persevere when the odds are stacked against you, the courage to face your inner demons, and the determination to rise above challenges. It is a testament to the idea that success is not just about personal achievement but about using one's success to make a positive impact on the world.

As you delve into the chapters of "A Journey of Resilience," may you find inspiration, hope, and a profound belief in the potential that lies within every individual. May you be reminded that, like Alexy, each of us possesses the capacity to turn adversity into opportunity and to build a brighter future, not only for ourselves but for those around us.

So, open this book with an open heart, for within these pages, you will discover the remarkable story of a young boy who dared to dream, who faced life's challenges head-on, and who, through his journey, teaches us all that resilience is the key to unlocking the extraordinary within us.

Preface

in the following pages, you will embark on a journey, one of unwavering resilience. This is the story of Alexy, a boy from a remote village, who defied the odds and transformed his life. His journey is a testament to the strength of the human spirit, a reminder that determination and hope can overcome any challenge. Join us as we explore the remarkable story of Alexy's life

Acknowledgements

I would like to express my heartfelt gratitude to all those who made this book possible. First and foremost, to the incredible individuals who shared their stories, wisdom, and experiences, thank you for allowing me to weave them into the tapestry of Alexy's journey.

To the mentors, friends, and loved ones who inspired and supported Alexy along his path, your roles in shaping this narrative are immeasurable. Your unwavering belief in the power of resilience and determination shines through these pages.

A special thank you to the countless teachers, educators, and mental health professionals who work tirelessly to empower individuals and communities. Your dedication to nurturing young minds and fostering emotional well-being is truly commendable.

I would also like to extend my appreciation to the readers, whose curiosity and thirst for knowledge bring stories like this to life. Your engagement and enthusiasm fuel the creation of meaningful narratives.

Lastly, to the authors, editors, and publishers who help transform words into stories, I am grateful for your expertise and commitment to the craft of storytelling.

This book is a collaborative effort, a tapestry woven together by the experiences and contributions of many. Thank you for being a part of Alexy's journey of resilience.

Prologue

In the quiet corners of a remote village, amidst the whispers of the forest and the rustling leaves, there lived a young boy named Alexy. His story, like many others, began with humble beginnings, but it was destined to be anything but ordinary. As we embark on this journey through the pages of his life, we'll witness the trials, triumphs, and transformations of a boy who defied the odds to become a beacon of resilience and hope. This is a story of dreams woven against the backdrop of challenges, of unwavering determination in the face of adversity, and of the enduring power of the human spirit. Welcome to the extraordinary journey of Alexy—a journey of resilience.

"The Remarkable Alexy"

In a faraway village near a big forest, life was hard for the Sharma family. Alexy, the oldest son, was a shining light in their struggles. The Sharmas were a simple family that didn't have much. Alexy's dad worked as a laborer, and his mom sewed clothes for a living. They had a little girl named Anna who was too young to understand their difficulties.

Even though they didn't have much money, the Sharmas had something special – love for each other. They cared deeply for one another and helped each other when times were tough. Their small house may not have been fancy, but it was full of love.

What made Alexy stand out was his big heart and his love for learning. He was an excellent student, even though his village school didn't have many resources. He was not only smart but also kind, and he always wanted to help others.

Every evening, after helping his dad with work and his mom with sewing, Alexy would sit under a tree near their home. He loved to read books borrowed from the village library. He would get lost in the stories and dream of a better future for his family.

The village saw something special in Alexy, not just as a student but as a young businessman. He was good at trading and making deals to help his family. He also knew how to talk to people and make friends. His kindness made everyone like him, and soon, he became the heart of the village.

As the sun set and the sky turned orange, Alexy's dreams grew brighter. He knew that education was the key to making life better for his family. He was determined to work hard for it. The Sharmas, living near the big forest, found strength in their togetherness and the dreams that Alexy had for them.

The title of this chapter could be "The Remarkable Alexy," showing how Alexy's unique qualities and his family's love helped them face tough times and look towards a brighter future. It's a story about not giving up and believing in the power of education and love, no matter the challenges

CHAPTER TWO

"Alexy's Journey Begins"

One day, a golden opportunity knocked on Alexy's door. Some kind mentors from his village's upper primary school alumni learned about his extraordinary potential and decided to help him. They saw his determination and gifted him a chance to study more about technology and business. It was a dream come true for Alexy.

As Alexy started to explore this new world of learning, his eyes sparkled with excitement. The mentors taught him about computers, the internet, and how they could be used to create amazing things. Alexy soaked up this knowledge like a sponge, eager to grasp every bit of it.

But, back in the village, people began to worry. They thought technology was a dangerous thing, and they feared what might happen if a young boy like Alexy got too involved with it. Some whispered that he might lose touch with his roots, forgetting the simple life they all cherished.

However, Alexy's heart remained as kind as ever. He understood his people's concerns and decided to use his newfound knowledge for the betterment of his village. With the support of his mentors, he hatched a plan to bridge the gap between technology and the simplicity of village life.

He started by teaching basic computer skills to the children of the village, turning a small hut into a makeshift computer center. The children were fascinated by the world of computers and the endless possibilities they offered. Alexy's act of kindness not only brought a sense of wonder but also a glimmer of hope to the village.

The title of this chapter could be "Alexy's Journey Begins," signifying the start of his exciting adventure into the world of technology and business, as well as the challenges he faced when his village was hesitant about embracing this new path. It's a story about how one young boy's dreams and his determination to give back to his community can inspire change and hope.

"City Dreams"

The day finally came when Alexy had to leave his cozy village and head to the bustling city for his higher studies. With a heavy heart, he bid farewell to his family and friends, promising to return one day and make them proud.

Accompanied by some of his village friends, Alexy embarked on a journey to the city of opportunities. Everything in the city was different from what he had known. Tall buildings touched the sky, and the streets were crowded with people from all walks of life. The food, the culture, the pace of life—it was all new and exciting, yet overwhelming.

As they settled into their new lives, Alexy and his friends faced many challenges. The city was fast-paced, and they had to adapt quickly. They struggled with their studies at first, but their determination pushed them to work harder than ever. With time, they became not just students but also young entrepreneurs in the making.

The city presented endless possibilities. Alexy and his friends, inspired by their mentor's teachings back in the village, decided to start their own small business. They realized that the city dwellers were always on the go, and there was a demand for convenient, homemade snacks. So, they began making and selling traditional village snacks in the heart of the city.

Their business venture was challenging, but it brought them closer together and taught them valuable lessons about teamwork and perseverance. They worked tirelessly, balancing their studies with their business, often staying up late into the night.

The city, with all its complexities, also had a way of changing people. As Alexy and his friends navigated the bustling streets and diverse cultures, they grew wiser and more mature. They learned the value of hard work, adaptability, and the importance of staying true to their roots.

This chapter could be titled "City Dreams," highlighting Alexy and his friends' journey from a humble village to a vibrant city, where they faced new challenges, discovered new opportunities, and began building their own future. It's a story of growth, friendship, and the pursuit of dreams in an unfamiliar yet promising environment.

CHAPTER FOUR

"Alexy's School Days"

Life in the new, technical school was a far cry from what Alexy and his friends were used to in the village. The school was renowned for its rigor and high standards. Students there were some of the brightest young minds in the country, and many came from wealthy backgrounds. Alexy and his friends felt like small fish in a vast, competitive pond.

Academically, Alexy wasn't at the top of the class like some of his peers. But what set him apart was his entrepreneurial spirit. He had a vision and a dream to make a difference, and that made him stand out. People started to notice him not for his grades, but for his determination and ambition.

Alexy earned the tagline "Young Entrepreneur" in his school. Everyone knew he came from a remote forest area, and they admired his drive to build his dream despite the odds. The school was buzzing with talk about this boy from a far-off village who was going to change the world.

Even though Alexy was somewhat introverted in public, within his circle of friends, he was an extrovert. He had found a brotherhood among his friends who shared his dreams and goals. They motivated each other to keep pushing forward, even when the road seemed tough.

Alexy realized that to achieve his dreams, he needed more than just book smarts. He needed to develop his personal skills and build his brand. So, he started working on his communication skills. He learned how to network, how to speak confidently, and how to present his ideas effectively. It wasn't easy, but Alexy was determined to become not just a dreamer but a doer.

As time passed, Alexy's reputation continued to grow. His journey was a testament to the power of determination and resilience. In this challenging school, he was learning not just from textbooks but from life itself. And through it all, he was building the foundation for something extraordinary.

The title of this chapter could be "Alexy's School Days," highlighting the challenges and growth he experienced in the highly competitive and technical school, where he stood out not for his academic brilliance but for his unwavering determination to chase his dreams. It's a story of self-discovery, friendship, and the transformative power of ambition.

CHAPTER FIVE

"The Rollercoaster of Emotions"

After Alexy completed his Plus One exams, life took an unexpected turn. It was a time of both newfound opportunities and challenging emotions.

With his growing presence on social media, Alexy had started to share his story with the world. His journey from a remote village to a prestigious technical school had captured the hearts of many. His inspiring tale resonated with people, and slowly but surely, he began to gain recognition online. He became a small celebrity, admired by those who followed his journey.

But life has a way of throwing curveballs, and the Plus One exam results were one such curveball for Alexy. His grades were lower than he had hoped, and some people, unaware of his incredible journey, began to mock him. They judged him based solely on those grades, not realizing the depth of his determination and the hurdles he had overcome.

Alexy was emotionally sensitive, and these harsh judgments hit him hard. He struggled to cope with the pressure and the disappointment of not meeting his own expectations. His mood swings became more pronounced, and there were moments when he found it difficult to handle the overwhelming emotions.

In the midst of this emotional storm, Alexy retreated to the solitude of his dark hostel room. Every day, he found solace in the tears that flowed as he grappled with his feelings of inadequacy and self-doubt. It was a challenging time for him, and he needed space to come to terms with the disappointment.

This chapter could be titled "The Rollercoaster of Emotions," depicting the highs and lows that Alexy experienced during this pivotal moment in his life. It's a story of vulnerability, the weight of expectations, and the importance of taking a pause when faced with adversity.

CHAPTER SIX

"Rising from the Shadows"

In the midst of his emotional turmoil, Alexy found strength in the people who truly cared about him. His beautiful friends from school and his loving girlfriend, Hendria, became his pillars of support. They saw beyond the grades and understood the incredible journey he had been on. With their unwavering love and encouragement, they helped him gradually begin to heal.

Alexy's friends never left his side. They listened when he needed to talk, and they gave him the space to be himself. Their laughter and camaraderie lifted his spirits, reminding him that he was not alone in his struggles. Hendria, in particular, held a special place in his heart. Her love and understanding provided him with the strength to face his demons.

As time passed, Alexy improved, but he wasn't completely out of the darkness yet. He recognized that he needed professional help to deal with his emotional challenges. It was a difficult step to take, but he knew it was necessary for his well-being.

With the support of his mentors, whom he trusted like family, Alexy shared his problems. They didn't judge him;

instead, they embraced him with compassion and encouraged him to seek help. Together, they decided to take Alexy to a hospital to see a psychologist and psychiatrist who could provide the guidance and treatment he needed.

At the hospital, Alexy met Dr. Roberts, a kind and understanding psychologist, and Dr. Miller, a skilled psychiatrist. Through therapy and counseling, Alexy began to unpack his emotional burdens. He learned coping strategies and ways to manage his mood swings. It was a challenging journey, but Alexy was determined to regain control of his emotions.

As the days turned into weeks, Alexy gradually emerged from the shadows that had enveloped him. The love of his friends, the unwavering support of Hendria, and the guidance of his mentors and the healthcare professionals became the guiding lights that helped him find his way back to a place of emotional stability.

The title of this chapter could be "Rising from the Shadows," symbolizing Alexy's journey to overcome his emotional challenges with the help of his loved ones and the support of professionals. It's a story of resilience, friendship, and the importance of seeking help when facing mental health struggles.

CHAPTER SEVEN

"The Return of the Resilient"

With newfound strength and determination, Alexy returned to his school, his spirit unwavering. He chose not to burden his family with the pain he had been through; instead, he focused on keeping them strong.

As he stepped back into the school, his behavior showed subtle signs of his past struggles. But his friends, including his ever-supportive girlfriend, Hendria, were by his side, ready to help him overcome any hurdles that lay ahead. They understood the battles he fought within, and they offered unwavering support, helping him find his way back to his old self.

One person who played a pivotal role in Alexy's recovery was his class teacher. She had grown fond of Alexy's character and saw the potential in him. Knowing his journey and his struggles, she began to overcare for him, showering him with kindness and support. Her love for Alexy was so strong that he started calling her "mamma," a term of endearment that was initially met with surprise but soon shocked by everyone.

Despite her high position and reputation for being stern, Alexy's "mamma" had a soft spot for him. Her warmth and guidance helped him rebuild his confidence. Alexy's business journey, which had been put on hold during his difficult times, slowly gained momentum once again. With the support of his friends, the love of Hendria, and the care of his beloved teacher, Alexy's life began to fall back into place.

Through his journey of resilience, Alexy learned that it's okay to seek help when needed, and that true strength lies not only in overcoming challenges but also in leaning on the love and support of those who care about you.

The title of this chapter could be "The Return of the Resilient," reflecting Alexy's comeback to his school, his renewed determination, and the unwavering support of those who stood by his side. It's a story of recovery, friendship, and the power of love and mentorship in the face of adversity.

"The Unspoken Dilemma"

Alexy's relationship with his teacher, whom he affectionately called "mamma," was a special bond that had grown stronger over time. She had taken him under her wing, providing unwavering support and care. Alexy was not just a student to her; he was like a son, someone she could confide in.

Alexy had always been a good listener, and "mamma" found solace in sharing her thoughts and concerns with him. She told him about her dreams, her struggles, and even her deepest secrets. She trusted him implicitly, and Alexy held her words close to his heart.

But with time, an unspoken dilemma began to weigh on Alexy's shoulders. He could sense that "mamma" loved him unconditionally, and while he deeply cared for her in return, he was aware of the boundaries that should exist between a teacher and a student.

As "mamma" continued to confide in him, Alexy faced a moral quandary. He wondered if it was fair to be privy to her personal struggles and intimate thoughts. He worried that their close relationchip might be causing her harm, as she poured her heart out to him.

Alexy's kindness and empathy were his strengths, but they also posed a challenge. He knew he needed to address this delicate situation, not only for his own peace of mind but also for the well-being of his beloved teacher.

In the midst of his own journey of resilience and self-discovery, Alexy decided to have an honest conversation with "mamma." He expressed his gratitude for her support and the love she had shown him but gently conveyed his concerns about the boundaries of their relationship.

The conversation was difficult, but it was also cathartic. "Mamma" understood Alexy's perspective and appreciated his maturity in handling the situation. She assured him that her love and care for him would never waver, but she also recognized the need for a more balanced student-teacher relationship.

Their bond remained strong, and Alexy continued to thrive in his studies and personal growth. The unspoken dilemma had been addressed, and both Alexy and "mamma" had learned valuable lessons about boundaries, trust, and the complexities of love.

The title of this chapter could be "The Unspoken Dilemma," highlighting the emotional challenges Alexy faced as he navigated his unique relationship with his teacher and the importance of addressing sensitive issues for the sake of personal growth and healthy relationships.

CHAPTER NINE

"Unmasking the Pain"

Despite the deep trust and affection Alexy had for his teacher, "Mamma," a shadow began to loom over their relationship. Mamma's behavior towards him took an unexpected and distressing turn. She began treating him with rudeness and, at times, a hint of lustfulness, which left him bewildered and deeply hurt.

Alexy chose to suffer in silence. He hid the pain that this sudden change in his teacher's demeanor caused him, shielding his family and friends from this disturbing reality. He knew mamma had two children around his age, and perhaps her own personal struggles had clouded her judgment and affected her behavior towards him.

Months passed, and Alexy wrestled with this emotional turmoil in solitude. He tried to rationalize her actions, believing that forgiveness was the path to healing. But the pain festered within him, hidden behind a facade of strength and resilience.

Then, one fateful day, a chance encounter with Mamma triggered a traumatic response within him. The flood of emotions and memories overwhelmed him, and he could no longer contain the trauma he had been concealing. His mental state deteriorated rapidly, leading to a crisis that required immediate attention.

Alexy was hospitalized for seventeen long days. During this time, he underwent intensive treatment, therapy, and counseling. The doctors and mental health professionals worked tirelessly to help him confront and process the pain he had hidden for so long.

Slowly but surely, Alexy began to heal. The treatment allowed him to address the trauma, release the pent-up emotions, and rebuild his emotional well-being. With the support of his healthcare team, his family, and his friends, he emerged from this challenging chapter with newfound strength and resilience.

This chapter could be titled "Unmasking the Pain," reflecting Alexy's journey to confront the trauma he had endured in silence and the steps he took to heal and recover. It's a story of resilience, the importance of seeking help when needed, and the power of healing from emotional wounds.

CHAPTER TEN

"The Journey to Success and Giving Back"

As Alexy continued his personal and academic journey, he realized that overcoming his challenges had made him stronger. With the unwavering support of his loving mentors, he charted a path toward his dreams. His journey was filled with hard work, determination, and a relentless pursuit of his goals.

In his pursuit of success, Alexy faced moments of loss. Important people came and went from his life, leaving behind valuable lessons and memories. While these departures were bittersweet, they taught him the importance of resilience and adapting to change. He learned to cherish the moments he had with people, knowing that life's journey was marked by both arrivals and departures.

With time, Alexy's hard work paid off, and he emerged as a multi-billionaire in the world of business. His family, who had once struggled to make ends meet, now lived comfortably and happily. They celebrated Alexy's achievements, not just for his financial success but for his unwavering determination to create a better life for them all.

But Alexy's journey didn't end with personal success. He believed in giving back to the world that had nurtured his dreams. Inspired by his own experiences, he founded a non-profit charity organization dedicated to helping underprivileged students access quality education. He knew that education was the key to breaking the cycle of poverty, and he wanted to provide opportunities for others, just as he had received them.

Alexy's philanthropic efforts didn't stop there. He also extended his support to people facing mental health struggles, recognizing the importance of mental well-being. Through counseling services and awareness programs, he aimed to empower individuals to seek help and find the strength to overcome their challenges.

Additionally, Alexy was passionate about women's empowerment. He believed that women had the potential to be successful entrepreneurs and leaders. Through mentorship programs and financial support, he encouraged women to pursue their entrepreneurial dreams, contributing to a more equal and inclusive society.

In the end, Alexy's journey was not just about personal success, but about making a positive impact on the world. He had risen above his challenges, overcome adversity, and now, he was dedicated to helping others do the same. His story was a testament to the power of determination, resilience, and the desire to create a better world for all.

The title of this chapter could be "The Journey to Success and Giving Back," encapsulating Alexy's remarkable journey from hardship to success and his commitment to making a difference in the lives of others.

"a Journey Of Resilience"

In the pages of this book, we've followed the remarkable journey of Alexy, a young boy from a remote village, whose life was marked by challenges, dreams, and unwavering determination. As we reach the conclusion of this story, we find ourselves reflecting on the lessons learned and the enduring spirit of resilience.

Alexy's life was a testament to the power of hope and the ability to rise above adversity. From his humble beginnings in a village near the forest to his struggles in a technical school, and from his emotional challenges to his triumphs as a multi-billionaire entrepreneur, Alexy's journey was a rollercoaster of experiences and emotions.

Through it all, one thing remained constant: Alexy's indomitable spirit. He faced hurdles that would have left many defeated, but he emerged stronger and more determined each time. His journey was not without pain, but it was also filled with love, friendship, and the unwavering support of those who believed in him.

Alexy's story serves as a reminder that success is not defined solely by material wealth but by the courage to chase one's dreams, the resilience to overcome setbacks, and the compassion to give back to the world. He built a legacy not only through his business empire but also through the non-profit charity organization that helped underprivileged students, supported those facing mental health challenges, and empowered women to become entrepreneurs.

The title of this book, "The Hidden Gem of the Forest ," encapsulates the essence of Alexy's story—a tale of a young boy who faced adversity with unwavering determination, turning challenges into stepping stones toward a brighter future.

As we close the book on Alexy's journey, may his story inspire us all to embrace resilience, pursue our dreams, and make a positive impact on the world, no matter where we come from or what challenges we may face. Alexy's journey is a testament to the extraordinary potential that lies within each of us, waiting to be discovered and shared with the world.